The Berenstain Bears'
Fall Family Fun

Stan & Jan Berenstain

Random House New York

Compilation and cover art copyright © 2012 by Berenstain Enterprises, Inc.

All rights reserved. Published in the United States by Random House Children's Books, a division of Penguin Random House LLC, New York.

The stories in this collection were originally published separately in the United States by Random House Children's Books as the following:

The Berenstain Bears: Trick or Treat copyright © 1989
by Berenstain Enterprises, Inc.

The Berenstain Bears and the Prize Pumpkin copyright © 1990
by Berenstain Enterprises, Inc.

Random House and the colophon are registered trademarks
of Penguin Random House LLC.

Visit us on the Web!
rhcbooks.com
BerenstainBears.com

Educators and librarians, for a variety of teaching tools, visit us at
RHTeachersLibrarians.com

ISBN: 978-1-9848-4766-9

Printed in the United States of America   10 9 8 7 6 5 4 3 2 1

Contents

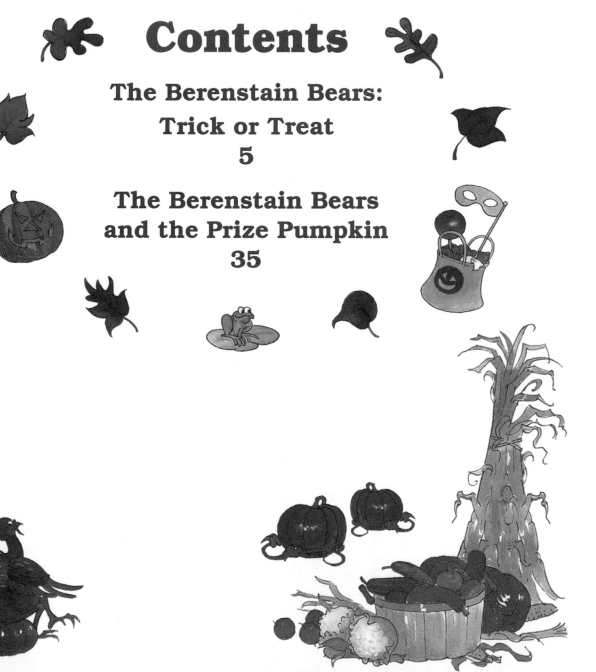

The Berenstain Bears
TRICK OR TREAT

Even little bears
expect a good fright
when they go out for treats
on Halloween night.

The sights and sounds of autumn
were all around as Mama Bear pushed her
shopping cart along the path that led
to the Bear family's tree house.

The trees and shrubs were ablaze with color. Farmer Ben's pumpkins stood bright orange in the October sun. The crows cawed noisily as they searched the stubble for bits of corn. Wild geese in great V-formations honked high in the sky as they flew south.

But the surest sign of the season was inside the tree house hiding behind Papa Bear's easy chair. It was Brother Bear waiting to try out his Halloween costume on Mama. It wasn't Halloween yet, but Brother and Sister couldn't wait to try on their new costumes. Sister was going to be a beautiful ballerina. "Well, what do you think?" she asked, taking the third position.

"Shh!" said Brother. "Mama's coming!" Brother had chosen to be a spooky monster on Halloween. He had bought the spookiest monster mask he could find, and Mama made the rest of the costume.

"Boo!" he shouted as Mama
came in with the groceries.

"Help! A monster!" she
cried, pretending to be
frightened.

"It's only me, Mama," he
said, showing his face.

"So it is," said Mama.
"Well, that just goes to
show that appearances can
be deceiving."

"Appearances can be deceiving—
what's that mean?" asked Sister.

"It's just a grown-up way of saying that
things aren't always what they look like,"
explained Mama as she unpacked the groceries.

"Look! Goodies!" said Brother.

"Hands off, please," said Mama. "Those
are for trick-or-treaters who come
to our house tomorrow
night."

Brother and Sister were very excited about Halloween—and a little nervous, too. This was the first year they would be going trick-or-treating without a grown-up along to supervise. "I'm not so sure I like the idea of them going by themselves," said Papa as he carved the pumpkin he got from Farmer Ben.

"It's pretty spooky out there,"
he added, making a scary face
at the cubs.

"Now, Papa," said Mama. "If Brother and Sister want to accept the challenge of going out on their own, I think we should encourage them.

"But remember," she continued, turning to the cubs, "there'll be strict rules: you'll stay in your own neighborhood and you won't eat any of the treats until you're back home."

"Besides," said Brother, "we won't really be by ourselves. We made a trick-or-treat date with Cousin Freddy, Lizzy Bruin, and Queenie McBear."

15

"There!" said Papa, putting the finishing touches on the jack-o'-lantern. Then he lit a candle inside it and turned out all the lights. It was pretty scary.

The next day Brother and Sister began planning the trick-or-treat route they'd follow that night. Brother got a pencil and paper and made a map of the neighborhood. That way, he explained, they wouldn't miss anybody. "Let's see, now," he said, "we'll stop at our houses first—ours, Freddy's, Lizzy's, and Queenie's. Then we'll do Farmer Ben's and our sitter's— Mrs. Grizzle."

"Mrs. Grizzle, for sure," agreed Sister. "She usually makes special Halloween cookies."

"And Teacher Jane—she gives out good stuff. How about Dr. Grizzly?" asked Brother. "She's into health snacks."

"I think so—just to be polite," said Sis.

"Gramps and Gran, of course."

"Of course."

TRICK-OR-TREAT MAP

"I'll tell you one place we *are* going to miss," said Brother, folding his map.

"What place is that?" asked Sister.

"That one!" he answered, pointing out the window at the home of old Miz McGrizz. It was a spooky, twisted old tree house in a thicket at the end of Crooked Lane. "We're definitely not going there," he added with a shiver.

"Whyever not?" asked Mama, who was listening.

"Why not?" said the cubs. "Because she's a witch! That's why not!"

"What utter nonsense!" protested Mama. "True, Miz McGrizz is old and bent and rather forbidding-looking. But I can assure you she's a perfectly nice person." But the cubs didn't believe her. Not for a minute. They knew better. *Everybody* knew better. No doubt about it, Miz McGrizz was a witch, for sure.

Just after dark, a pirate, a skeleton, and the Wicked Queen from *Snow White* came for Brother and Sister.

They were Freddy, Lizzy,
and Queenie, of course, and
together they ventured out
into the darkness with their
trick-or-treat bags.

Before they could get started collecting Halloween goodies, they were joined by some worrisome company: Too-Tall Grizzly and his gang, out for mischief. Too-Tall didn't waste any time trying to get Brother, Sister, and their friends to go along with him and his gang.

"Come on. We'll show you goody-goodies how to have some *real* Halloween fun," he said, pulling Brother along with him.

"What sort of fun?" asked Brother warily.

"Oh, you might say we're gonna put the trick back in trick or treat," he said, chuckling. It was so dark that Brother and the others didn't notice where they were heading.

"Hey!" said Sister. "This is Crooked Lane!"

"That's right," said Too-Tall. "We're gonna play a few tricks on old Witch McGrizz."

"W-what sort of tricks?" asked Brother. Her gnarled, twisted old tree house loomed ahead.

"First," whispered Too-Tall, taking a roll of toilet paper from his jacket, "we'll decorate her house with a little of this. Then maybe we'll tie a few knots in her clothesline. Then smear some honey on her broomstick so she'll stick to it when she tries to fly."

But before Too-Tall and his gang could start their mischief, the front door opened and a bright yellow light stabbed the darkness. And there in the doorway stood the frightening figure of old Miz McGrizz! "Aha!" she said in a gravelly voice. "I'm ready for you!"

She then led the terrified cubs into a cozy living room. To their great surprise, there was a big tray of beautiful candy apples all prepared for Halloween visitors.

"Mama was right," whispered Sister to Brother. "Miz McGrizz really *is* a sweet, kind old person!"

The cubs thanked her for the beautiful apples and went about the rest of their trick-or-treat business.

Later that evening Brother and Sister were at home looking over all the treats they had collected. The beautiful candy apples stood out, and Papa asked where they came from.

"From Miz McGrizz," answered Brother.

"From that scary-looking old grouch-puss that lives down Crooked Lane?" said Papa.

"That's right," said Brother, taking a delicious bite of his candy apple.

"You must really try to remember, Papa," said Sister, giving her apple a little lick, "appearances can be quite deceiving."

The Berenstain Bears
and the
PRIZE PUMPKIN

1st Prize, 2nd Prize,
3rd Prize or none—
At Thanksgiving time,
more than a contest
is won.

"Pumpkins are just like everything else in nature," said Papa Bear as he and the cubs finished weeding the pumpkin patch. "No two of them are exactly alike."

"That's for sure," agreed Brother Bear. "Look at that funny flat one and that lumpy one over there." Then there was the Giant, which is what Papa had named one that just seemed to be getting bigger and bigger.

"Why is it that no two things are exactly alike?" asked Sister Bear.

"It's just the way nature is," answered Papa.

"Time to wash up
for supper!" called
Mama Bear from the
tree house steps.

"What about Queenie McBear's twin brothers?" asked Sister.

"They certainly look a lot alike," said Papa. "But I've noticed that Mrs. McBear can tell them apart quite easily."

"In you go," said Mama, shooing her family into the house.

But Sister didn't go right in.
She stood on the stoop for a
moment and looked out over
Bear Country.

It was well into fall, so the days were getting shorter. Halloween had come and gone. Pretty soon the Bears would start thinking about Christmas. But right now Bear Country was aglow in the setting sun. Farmer Ben's well-kept farm looked especially fine, with its baled hay, corn shocks, and pumpkins casting long shadows.

"I guess nature's pretty amazing,"
Sister said as she looked out over
the beautiful scene.

"It's the most amazing thing
there is," said Mama. "Come
on now, in you go."

"Farmer Ben's farm sure looks beautiful in the setting sun," said Sister as the family sat down to supper.

"Humph!" said Papa grumpily. "Farmer Ben's not such a much."

"'Not such a much'?" said Mama. "Why, Ben is the finest farmer in Bear Country—and besides, he's one of your best friends."

"That may be so," said Papa. "But earlier today he came by and said, 'Nice little pumpkin patch you've got there, Papa.'"

"What he said is true," said Mama. "Especially compared to his fields and fields of pumpkins."

"That may be so, too," grumped Papa. "But I didn't like the way he said it— he sort of chuckled. My patch may be small, but the Giant is big. It may be the biggest and best pumpkin in all Bear Country. What do you think about that?"

"I think you're being
oversensitive," said Mama.
"Come, let's clear the table
so the cubs can do their
homework."

Brother and Sister sighed as they spread their books out on the table.

"What's that all about?" asked Papa.

"Oh, I was just thinking . . . ," said Brother. "With Halloween over and Christmas almost two months away, there's nothing to look forward to."

"That's right," added Sister. "Nothing except lots of homework."

"Oh, is that so?" protested Mama Bear.

"It just so happens that there's something very important to look forward to—a very special holiday called Thanksgiving. That's when we give thanks for all the wonderful—"

"Your mama's absolutely right," interrupted Papa.

He pointed to a notice in the evening paper. It said: Don't Forget This Year's Thanksgiving Festival! Entry Blanks for the Big Pumpkin Contest Available at City Hall!

"Thanksgiving's a *very* important holiday. Especially this year, because we're going to enter the Giant in the pumpkin contest and beat the pants off Farmer Ben!"

"But, Papa, he's a professional," said Brother. "He's won the contest ten years in a row!"

"All the more reason to teach him a lesson. Come on, let's go out and check up on the next heavyweight pumpkin champion of Bear Country!" he said.

47

Now it was Mama's turn to sigh. Thanksgiving was about giving thanks—not beating the pants off Farmer Ben.

"Isn't it a beauty?" Papa said after they admired the Giant. Across the road they could see a field of Ben's pumpkins. There were lots of fine ones, but none that measured up to the Giant.

"There's homework to be done!" called Mama Bear from the house. As they left, the cubs asked Papa, "Aren't you coming in?"

"Nope," he said. "I'm going to stay out here a little while and watch the Giant grow."

49

And grow it did. It grew bigger, rounder, and oranger every day.

When Papa and the cubs went to City Hall to get an entry blank for the contest, they saw the place where the winning pumpkin would go on display.

"We can't lose!" said Papa. In their mind's eye they could see their pumpkin in the place of honor.

CITY HALL

WATCH THIS SPOT FOR THE PRIZE PUMPKIN

Mama tried to remind them what Thanksgiving was really about, but every time she did, Papa would interrupt. "You'll have to excuse me, my dear," he'd say. "It's time to water the Giant."

He not only watered it on a regular schedule and gave it special plant food, but he also covered it with a blanket at night and tucked it in against the cold.

One afternoon, the cubs got off the school bus with something important to tell Papa, but they were stopped in their tracks by what they saw: he was *talking to the Giant.*

Mama explained that Papa had bought a book from the swindler Raffish Ralph about how to encourage your plants to grow by talking to them.

"Well," said Brother, "I don't suppose it can do any harm. . . ."

"It sure could harm his reputation," said Sister, "if anybody saw him talking to a pumpkin."

"Er, Papa," Brother said, "a cub at school told me he went on a class trip to Ben's farm and saw some pretty big pumpkins—especially one really big one that Ben calls the Monster."

"We've got to get a look at it," said Papa.

That evening Papa and the cubs climbed through the fence into Farmer Ben's field. They saw some good-sized pumpkins, but none to match the Giant.

"Maybe it's behind the barn," whispered Papa.

Suddenly a light shone on them and they heard Ben shout, "Prowlers in the pumpkin field! Get me my pitchfork!"

They got out of there so fast Papa tore his overalls climbing through the fence.

"What have you been up to?" asked Mama Bear when they got home.

"Nothing much," said Papa. "Just strolling in the moonlight!"

The weekend before Thanksgiving arrived, and it was time for the big festival. The Bear family got there just in time. The pumpkin judging was about to begin! There were many fine pumpkins in the contest. But Papa was sure that none could measure up to the Giant . . . *until he saw the Monster!* It was at least as big and round and orange as his pumpkin—and maybe, *just maybe,* a little bigger, rounder, and oranger.

The Bears waited nervously while the judges studied, measured, and weighed, and then studied, measured, and weighed some more. Finally, they made their announcement: "THE FIRST-PRIZE WINNER— *AND STILL CHAMPION . . .*"

Of course, that meant Farmer Ben had won. It was close—it turned out that Ben's Monster was just a little bigger, rounder, and oranger than Papa's Giant. But that wasn't the worst of it. The Giant didn't even come in second. A beautiful pumpkin grown by Miz McGrizz won second prize. The Giant came in third. Papa and the cubs were crushed . . . crushed and very quiet as they pushed their third-prize winner home.

It wasn't until they reached the crest of a hill that overlooked Bear Country that Mama decided to have her say. "I know you're disappointed. But third prize is nothing to be ashamed of. Besides, Thanksgiving isn't about contests and prizes. It's about giving thanks. And it seems to me that we have a lot to be thankful for."

Perhaps it was Mama's lecture, or maybe it was how beautiful Bear Country looked in the sunset's rosy glow. But whatever the reason, Papa and the cubs began to understand what Mama was talking about.

Even more so on Thanksgiving Day. After the Bears gave thanks for the wonderful meal they were about to enjoy, Sister Bear gave her own special thanks. "I'm thankful," she said, "that we *didn't* win first prize: if we had, the Giant would be on display in front of City Hall instead of being part of the yummy pies we're going to have for dessert!"

As the laughter faded and the Bears thought about the blessings of family, home, friends, and neighbors, they knew deep in their hearts that there was no question about it—indeed they did have a great deal to be thankful for.